A HAPPY ENDING BOOK ™

the New Baby

by Jane Carruth   illustrated by Tony Hutchings

MODERN PUBLISHING
A Division of Unisystems, Inc.
New York, New York 10022

To: Our Dear Granddaughter
Kacey Lee

From: Mamaw & Papaw

Love You

Tippu and his friend Monty were playing a game in the garden when Mommy appeared. She was pushing the carriage with Tippu's new baby sister in it. "All that noise!" she cried. "I'm afraid the baby will wake up."

Tippu scowled. "That baby spoils everything!" he muttered. But Mommy pretended not to hear.

"I won't be far away," she went on. "Just in the kitchen. But since it's such a nice day, I'm leaving the baby in the garden. So no more noisy games, Tippu—and if your little sister wakes up, come and tell me at once."

"You can't have any fun with a new baby around," grumbled Tippu, as his mother went indoors.

That night, while Mommy was busy ironing, Tippu asked
what they were going to do on the first day of his school
vacation. "You always take me somewhere special,"
he said.

"Not this time," said Mommy. "You know we can't leave
the baby on her own—" She stopped as Tippu's little sister
began crying in the next room. "She must need to be
changed," said Mommy. "Be a good boy and sort out the
ironing for me while I tend to her."

On Saturday Tippu went to the playground to meet
Monty. He was surprised to find that Monty had brought
along his little sister. "What a nuisance!" he exclaimed.
"Can't you take her home? Then we could have some real
fun on our own."

"Of course not," said Monty. "Besides, I like her."

"Please yourself," said Tippu crossly. "My baby sister is just a nuisance. I'll never like her!"

"Oh yes you will," said Monty. "You'll see!" Tippu refused to play with Monty and his sister. But he soon found it wasn't much fun whizzing down the slide all by himself.

Tippu always went roller-skating with Daddy on Saturday afternoons. Daddy liked him in his old play-clothes and didn't mind if his hair was untidy. "That baby can't spoil my roller-skating," Tippu told himself, as he went to tell Daddy he was ready.

"Sorry Tippu, no roller-skating today," said Daddy.
"Your Great Aunt Lucy is coming all the way from East
Woods with a present for your baby sister. And she will
want to see you, too."

But Tippu wasn't there when his Great Aunt Lucy arrived. She climbed out of her car with the presents, and Tippu's Mommy and Daddy went to meet her. "I just can't wait to see the new baby," she cried. "I suppose she's beautiful."

"She is," said Mommy. "We are both thrilled."

"She's just like her mother," said Daddy proudly.

"Where's my Tippu?" Great Aunt Lucy asked as they went indoors. "I have a present for him, too. I thought he would be here to welcome me."

"Oh, he's brushing his hair and making himself tidy for your visit," said Mommy.

"I want to see him first," said Great Aunt Lucy.

But Tippu didn't appear. "We had better look for him,"
said Great Aunt Lucy. "Perhaps he's playing hide and seek?"
Daddy looked in the kitchen and in the playroom. Then
he went outside and looked all around the garden and in
the shed. But Tippu was nowhere to be seen.

"I can't find him anywhere," Daddy said at last. Mommy began to look worried.

"Where can he be?" she said. "Why is he hiding from us?"

"Perhaps neither of you have been making a fuss over him since the new baby arrived," suggested Great Aunt Lucy. Mommy's eyes filled with tears.

The new baby was forgotten until, suddenly, they heard her crying. "She's in her crib upstairs," Daddy said. "I'll tend to her while you look for Tippu." He couldn't believe his eyes when he peeked around the door and saw Tippu!

"Stop crying," Tippu was saying. "I'm here. I'll take care of you." Daddy saw Tippu smile happily as his little sister stopped crying and smiled back at him. "Maybe Monty was right," Daddy heard him say. "I think I could like you, after all!"

Daddy crept downstairs. There was Great Aunt Lucy emptying out the closet hoping she would find Tippu hiding there. "He's upstairs with his baby sister," said Daddy. "He must have been hiding under our bed most for of the time."

"I'll go get him at once," Mommy cried joyfully. "I was beginning to think we had lost our precious Tippu forever!"

When Mommy went into the bedroom Tippu was looking pleased with himself. "I told her to go to sleep and she did," he said.

Mommy began hugging and kissing him. "Never mind the baby right now," she whispered. "My little boy matters too."

"I-I thought you loved the new baby more than me," Tippu whispered at last.

"How could you think that?" Mommy said softly. "We love you more than ever. It's just that our baby is so new and helpless."

After Great Aunt Lucy had had her tea, Tippu helped her open the presents. There was a brand-new toy car for him and a pretty hat for the baby. "Let me put her new hat on," Tippu cried. And Great Aunt Lucy nodded.

"What a lucky baby she is to have you to take care of her."

"I suppose she is!" said Tippu, as he smiled.